Let your
True Princess
heart shine as
a light for others
to follow –
Carol Ramos

Happy 8th
Birthday
Brianna!
Love your
Best friend
Mikayla
.P.S. I hope you
enjoy this
Book!

The True Princess™ *Series*

Elaine's Story

Written by
Carol Ranoa

Illustrated by
Gina Cruz-Rider

This book is dedicated to the original True Princesses,
Cheyenne, Calista and Olivia

Published in the United States 2010
by Aolani's Lair (subsidiary of The True Princess Series)
Temecula, California
Text © 2010 by The True Princess
Composed in the United States of America
Manufactured in China

Designed by Ruth Marcus

ISBN 978-0-578-06922-7

www.thetrueprincess.com

Long ago, and even in some parts
of our world today, there are kingdoms
ruled by Kings, Queens, Princesses and Princes
and their Royal Families. Usually it was expected
for royalty to marry each other. So a True Prince
was expected to marry a True Princess and so on
and so on and so on. And the only way to be a
True Princess was if you were born to a King and
Queen. Then Kings and Queens of other
Royal Families got together to arrange
marriages between their children.

Well things began to change

with a young Prince named Andre. Andre

believed that being a "true" princess or a "true"

prince meant more than just who your mother and father

were. So today, because of this story and other's,

anyone can become a "true" princess...

yes, even you! You'll understand

more as our story unfolds.

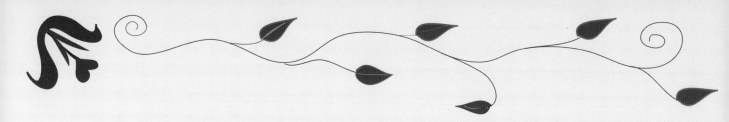

Prince Andre was very special
indeed. He was kind and loving and
of course, very, very handsome. All the
princesses in the kingdoms adored him and
wanted to be his bride. Many were beautiful.
Some were clever, and others were charming.
But with each meeting Andre felt that something was
missing. He had his own ideas. "Being beautiful
was just not enough. Clever and charming
were fun for just the moment." He wanted
to marry a princess that would be as
special on the inside as she looked
on the outside. He wanted a "true"
princess through and through.

"Just because your mother and father are King and Queen doesn't make someone a 'true' prince or princess. True royalty is kind and happy and leads with a gentle heart," he always said. "And a 'true' princess cares for the world around her. She cares deeply for all things in nature. Someday I will find my 'true' princess," Andre insisted. "Until that time, I will not marry."

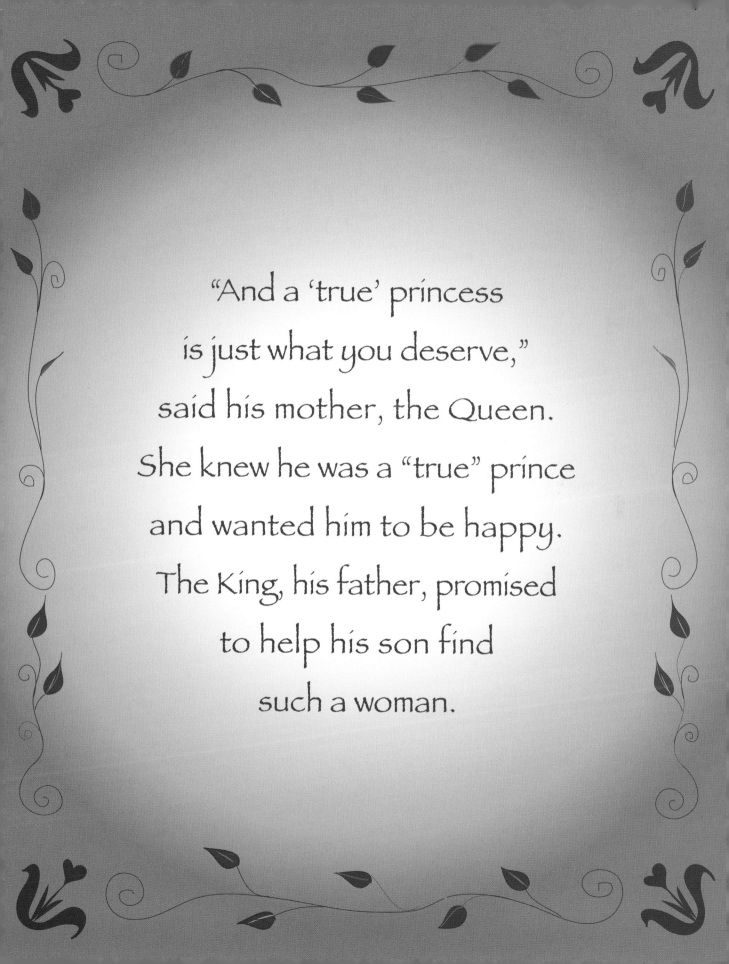

"And a 'true' princess
is just what you deserve,"
said his mother, the Queen.
She knew he was a "true" prince
and wanted him to be happy.
The King, his father, promised
to help his son find
such a woman.

Around the country
the young prince traveled
with his father on their Royal
Horses. They asked everyone in
every village, palace and castle
if they might know of the
whereabouts of a
"true" princess.

Well everyone thought
they did! They introduced the
Prince to many beautiful and talented
young ladies who all thought that the Prince
was very handsome indeed! Many wanted to
marry him right away! But as Andre tried to get to
know them, he didn't find a single "true" princess
amongst them. He found out that most of the beautiful
young women cared more about themselves than about
others. They wanted to sit and primp all day long.
They spent all their time combing their hair or picking
out beautiful dresses. They didn't even notice
the other people around them. In fact,
most were bossy to their friends, family
and servants. They just didn't care
about anything or anyone
but themselves.

Poor Prince Andre.
He was so sad.
"Why is it so hard to find
someone with a 'true' heart?

Someone who thinks about others
before she thinks about herself...
Someone who cares about the
happiness of others...
Someone who is kind and good
and looks for the goodness
in everyone."

With much disappointment
Prince Andre and his father
sadly returned home. Andre knew
in his heart that his "true" princess
was out there somewhere. He hoped
she was perhaps looking for him as well.
But where would he find her? "I believe
there are many young ladies who
are 'true' princesses in their
hearts. I just want to
find one!" he said.

The Royal Cook
tried to cheer Prince Andre up.
He made him his favorite dish for
supper. But Prince Andre didn't feel
like eating. He just stared sadly at the
plate. The Royal Jester tried to cheer
him up by telling him funny stories.
But Prince Andre didn't laugh.
His heart was sad and lonely.
He said "Thank you," but he
just couldn't find
the smiles.

Even the Royal Maids
put beautiful silken sheets on his
bed so he would sleep well. But he
didn't. He just tossed and turned all night.
His heart was not at peace. He dreamed of all
the wonderful things his "true" princess would
do. He dreamed of her teaching the young children
of the village. He thought of the things she would
do to be kind to our planet. He felt her
gratitude for all she had and for all the
people she would help. Many
sleepness nights passed.

One night a terrible storm suddenly appeared and
invaded the entire sky. It was so scary that everyone
in the kingdom stayed in their homes and shuttered their
windows as tightly as they could. No one dared travel about.
Violent winds howled through the trees as they twisted and gnarled
to the ground. Lightning pierced the black sky and was followed
by blasts of echoing thunder. It rained so hard that the land became
rivers and the rivers overflowed their banks. Prince Andre, his
mother, father and their servants could not sleep a wink.

Everyone huddled around
the fireplace trying to keep warm.
Between the cracks of thunder and howling
winds, there came a slight knock at the door.
It was such a gentle knock that at first no one
heard it. Soon it got loud enough for the family
to notice. Prince Andre walked over and opened
the door. He was shocked to find the most beautiful
young girl standing there. She had rain streaming
through her hair and down her face and water
running out of her shoes. She was shaking with cold.
"Good evening Your Majesty," she said politely.
"I am sorry to bother you on a night such as this but
I'm afraid I'm in a bit of a pickle...or should I say
puddle," as she looked down at her shoes. "I am
Princess Elaine from a kingdom beyond the forest.
I was out on an evening errand when the storm just
suddenly appeared. My coach got stuck in the
mud. My attendants went off to get help.
I fear they may have gotten lost in the
storm. Oh, I so hope they found shelter
and are warm. Would it be alright if I
rest up here a bit and wait for
the storm to pass?"

Prince Andre
could hardly speak.
He thought that she was the
loveliest thing he had ever seen, even
though she was dripping wet. She had
a gentleness about her that sent warm shivers
from the tips of his toes to the top of his head.
He felt his spirits lift as they hadn't in weeks.
He even felt he was taller. "Of course you
may stay," he said. "My handmaidens will
get you some towels and dry clothes
to change into. But why are you out
on a night such as this?"

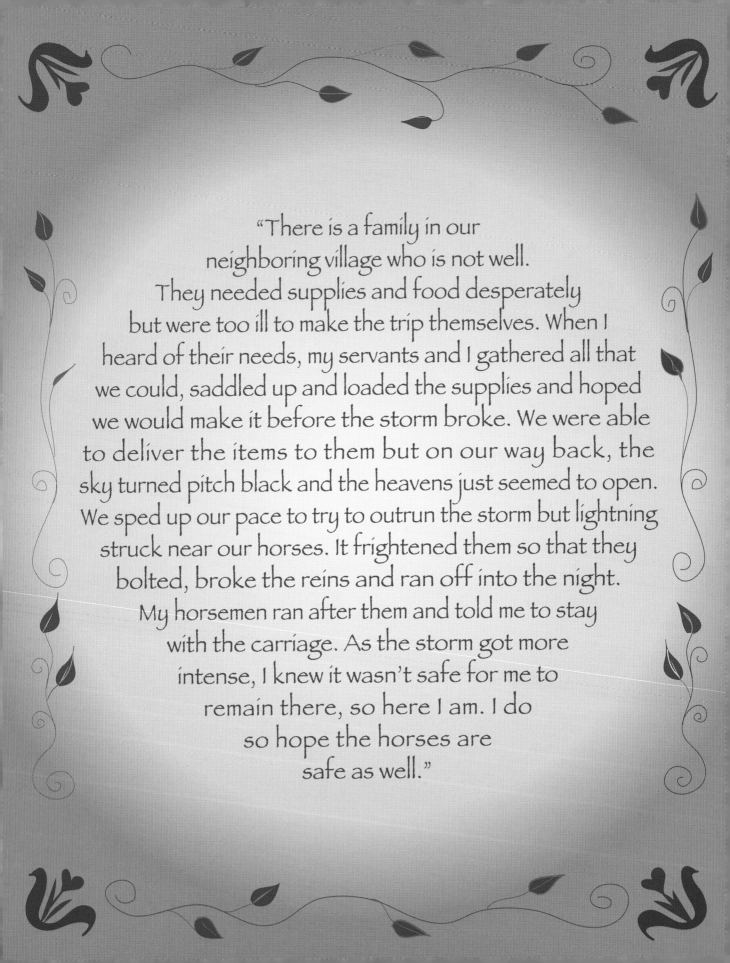

"There is a family in our
neighboring village who is not well.
They needed supplies and food desperately
but were too ill to make the trip themselves. When I
heard of their needs, my servants and I gathered all that
we could, saddled up and loaded the supplies and hoped
we would make it before the storm broke. We were able
to deliver the items to them but on our way back, the
sky turned pitch black and the heavens just seemed to open.
We sped up our pace to try to outrun the storm but lightning
struck near our horses. It frightened them so that they
bolted, broke the reins and ran off into the night.
My horsemen ran after them and told me to stay
with the carriage. As the storm got more
intense, I knew it wasn't safe for me to
remain there, so here I am. I do
so hope the horses are
safe as well."

Andre couldn't believe
his eyes or his ears. This beautiful
dripping girl put herself in danger just
to help a family in need. The thoughts
in his mind were echoing back to him.

A "true" princess cares about others.
A "true" princess doesn't give up.
A "true" princess is always ready to help.

"I wonder," he thought,
"if this could be the 'true'
princess I've been
looking for."

As if she read
his mind, the Queen got
up and said she was going
upstairs to get the bedroom ready
for Elaine. "We'll see if she's a 'true'
princess," the Queen thought. The
Queen understood her son's ideas
about a "true" princess. But she was
a bit old-fashioned and had her own
test to determine if someone was
indeed a "true" princess.

The Queen knew that a "true" princess was sensitive to the world in both her mind and her body. It was well-known in their Kingdom that a "true" princess could feel even the slightest speck of sand on the bottom of her shoe. So the Queen went into the bedroom with two servants and took the sheets and blankets off the bed.
On top of the mattress she placed a small dried pea.

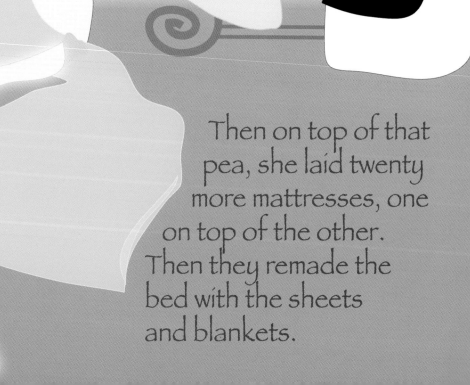

Then on top of that pea, she laid twenty more mattresses, one on top of the other. Then they remade the bed with the sheets and blankets.

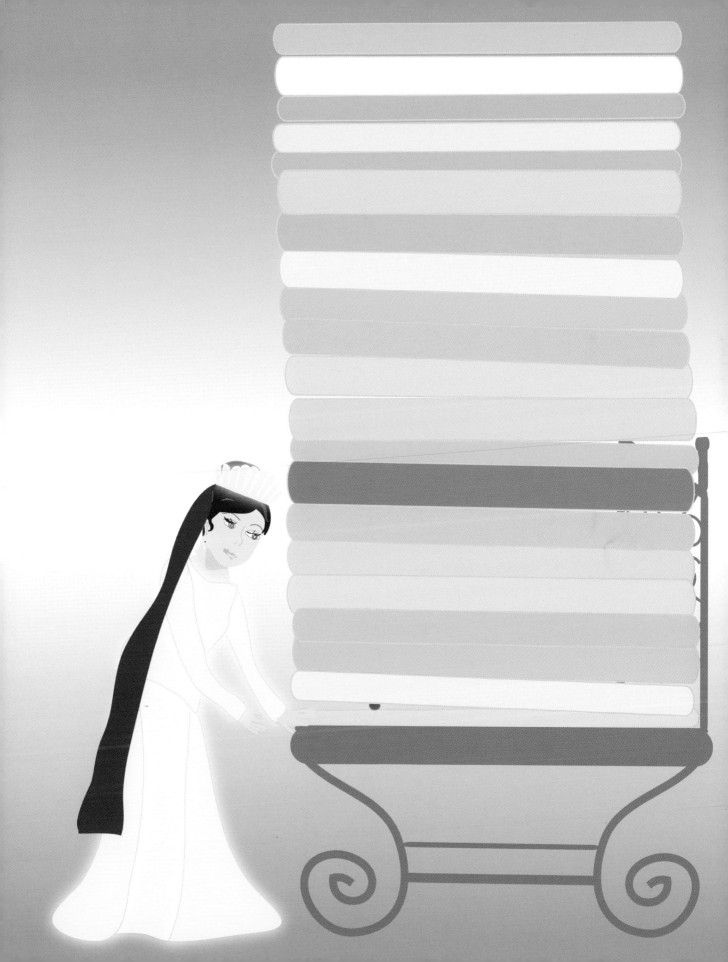

When Elaine came into the
bedroom, she was certainly surprised
by what she saw. But she would never dream
of being rude and questioning the Queen.
She truly respected her elders. She was
grateful for the dry clothes and warm bed to sleep
in, even if she had to climb a ladder to get into it.
Mostly she appreciated the kindness of this Royal
Family. As she climbed the ladder to the top
mattress, she glanced back down at the Queen
and said, "Thank you Your Majesty for your
kindness." "Goodnight" said the Queen.
"Sleep well." The Queen was most impressed
with this young lady. She was kind and
loving. She expressed gratitude and
appreciation. "I certainly hope she is a
'true' Princess," she thought.
"In the morning, we'll
know for sure."

Prince Andre did not sleep well. He tossed and turned all night while visions of the lovely Elaine danced in his head. She was kind. She was caring. Could she possibly be the "true" princess he had been looking for?

The King and Queen also felt how special Elaine was. All night they tossed and turned as well. "What if," they hoped "she was the 'true' princess of their son's dreams? That would make their son, Prince Andre, very happy."

But Princess Elaine's sleep was the least peaceful. She tossed back and forth all night. She couldn't find one inch of that bed that was comfortable.

She thought that it was probably because of the storm, losing her horses and worrying about her horsemen. She kept looking for the best position but it never was found. She couldn't wait for the sun to come up.

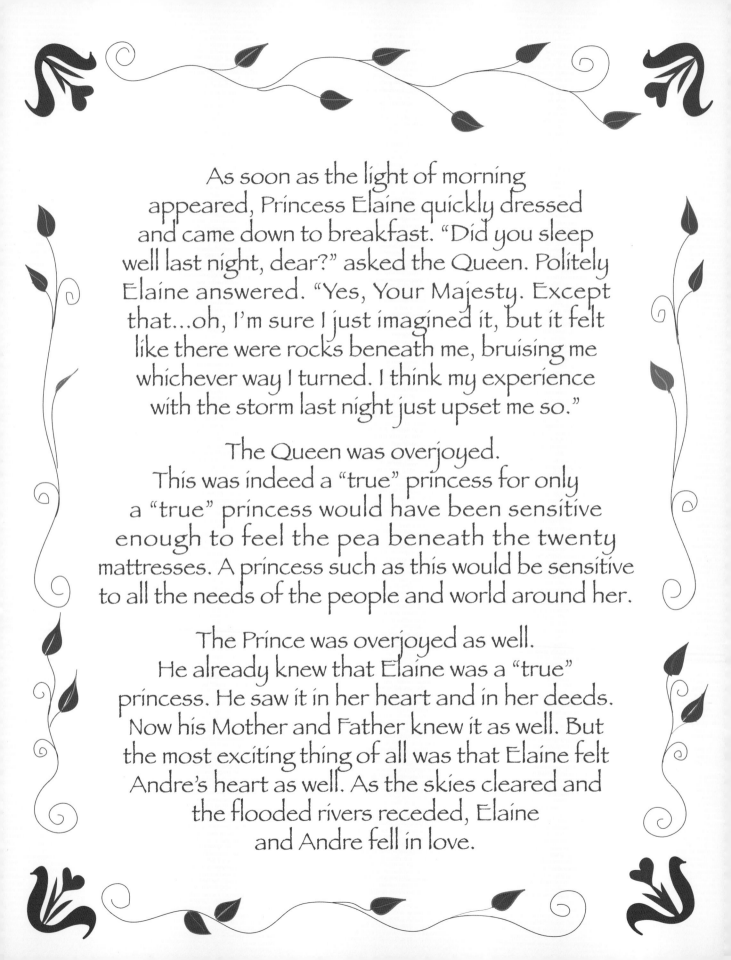

As soon as the light of morning
appeared, Princess Elaine quickly dressed
and came down to breakfast. "Did you sleep
well last night, dear?" asked the Queen. Politely
Elaine answered. "Yes, Your Majesty. Except
that...oh, I'm sure I just imagined it, but it felt
like there were rocks beneath me, bruising me
whichever way I turned. I think my experience
with the storm last night just upset me so."

The Queen was overjoyed.
This was indeed a "true" princess for only
a "true" princess would have been sensitive
enough to feel the pea beneath the twenty
mattresses. A princess such as this would be sensitive
to all the needs of the people and world around her.

The Prince was overjoyed as well.
He already knew that Elaine was a "true"
princess. He saw it in her heart and in her deeds.
Now his Mother and Father knew it as well. But
the most exciting thing of all was that Elaine felt
Andre's heart as well. As the skies cleared and
the flooded rivers receded, Elaine
and Andre fell in love.

Before the year ended,
Elaine and Andre were married.
They set out to live a life that comes
from having a "true" heart. They set an
example of goodness and giving for all.
Everyone in the Kingdom started being nicer
to each other. When help was needed, there
were many hands that were offered.
Even brothers and sisters
got along better.

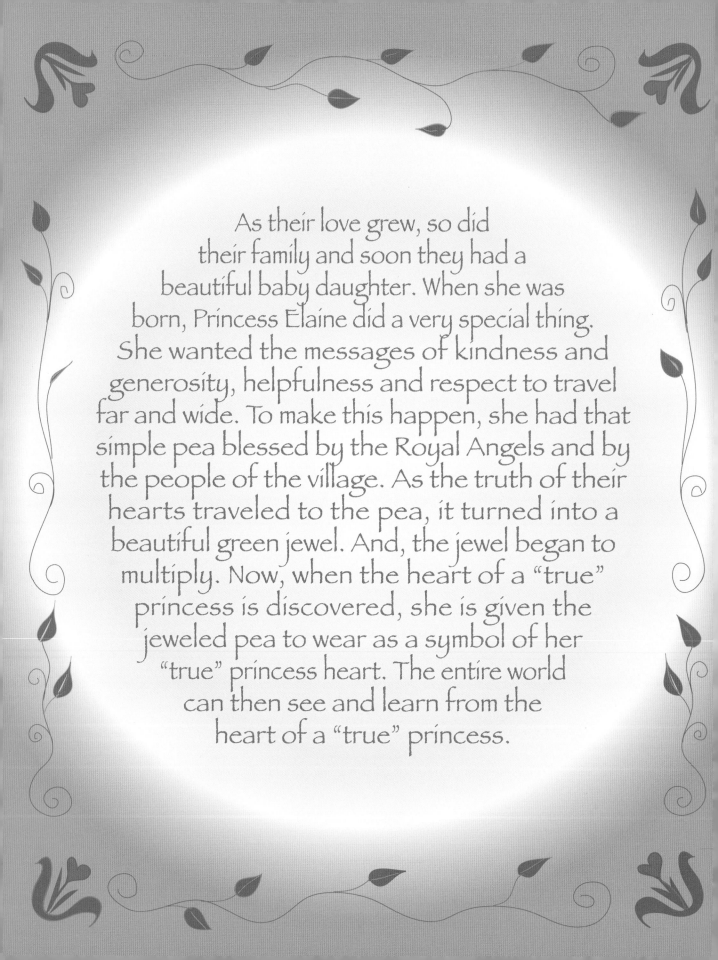

As their love grew, so did
their family and soon they had a
beautiful baby daughter. When she was
born, Princess Elaine did a very special thing.
She wanted the messages of kindness and
generosity, helpfulness and respect to travel
far and wide. To make this happen, she had that
simple pea blessed by the Royal Angels and by
the people of the village. As the truth of their
hearts traveled to the pea, it turned into a
beautiful green jewel. And, the jewel began to
multiply. Now, when the heart of a "true"
princess is discovered, she is given the
jeweled pea to wear as a symbol of her
"true" princess heart. The entire world
can then see and learn from the
heart of a "true" princess.

Are you a "true" princess,
worthy of wearing the jewel? Are
you kind to others? Do you show respect
to your parents and family? If you answer
YES to these questions, then we welcome
you to the Kingdom of the True Princess.
Come join us at www.thetrueprincess.com
where you can register for your jewel
and show the world your
True Princess Heart.